This book belongs to:

from darkness to light
from silence to singing
from stillness to dancing
from smallness to greatness
from frailty to might
transience to endurance
acorn to oak

For Sue and Tony, with love and thanks - S.H.
For Sue, Katy, Paul and David with love. - M.H.

The Furzey Oak

First published in the United Kingdom in 2008 by
The Clucket Press
220 Hill Lane
Southampton
Hants
SO15 7NR

www.tattybogle.com

isbn 13: 978-0-9549256-6-6

Layout and setting by Niall Horn
Printed in the United Kingdom by Borcombe SP, Romsey, Hampshire.

13579108642

THE FURZEY OAK

By

Sandra Horn   Mervyn Hathaway

The Clucket Press

Hundreds of years ago, in a high, windswept part
of the New Forest, a foraging jay pushed an acorn
into the ground and then forgot about it.

Slowly, as the years went by, the forgotten acorn grew into a sturdy tree.
It was bent and bowed by the wind, but its trunk was thick and strong
and it held a great mass of curving branches.

The oak was a shelter for many creatures.
Squirrels and birds built their nests among its leaves.
Beetles made homes beneath the bark.
Purple butterflies danced round its crown.

One night, there came a great storm.

A tearing, howling wind uprooted trees all through the forest.
It rocked the oak tree's roots and tore off some of its branches.

"It will have to come down," the foresters said,
"or it will fall anyway."

With axes and saws and ropes they felled the tree
and laid it along the ground.

"It's a bit stunted, eh?" one said, "T'wont be worth much."

"Ah, that's where you be wrong," said another.
"Look at them curves where the branches comes off; that'll make
the ribs of a fine ship — and there's plenty in the trunk for deck beams
and planks and treenails and such."

With a team of oxen, they dragged the tree out of the forest,
to a boatyard by the sea, where it was chopped and sawn
and carved into parts for a sailing ship.

She was named The Good Hope.

The Good Hope sailed the seas for many years.
The oak timbers were battered by the winds and the waves
and soaked in salt water.

Through it all, the oak wood stayed true.
The more it endured, the stronger it became.

Then, on a dark night in a bitter storm, the ship hit a rock
and broke her keel. Her crew clung to the oak decking
until they were rescued, but her sailing days were over.

She was hauled to shore and taken to pieces.
The beams and planks lay in the timber yard in rain
and frost and sun, until Bert Furzey came along.

"I'm looking for the right wood to build my house," he said,
"this here looks the very thing."

"You sure?" said his son, "some of it don't look quite straight,
to me."

"That don't matter!" said his father, "that's as strong as stone, that is
— and that don't come easy. It's coming through storms has made it
like that. Wood like that'll never fail."

 Bert and his son took the oak timbers back to the forest.

They built a cottage with snug rooms under the thatch.
The beams were curved, the stairs were uneven
and the floors were not quite flat, but the cottage stood firm
through season after season and all kinds of weather.

Once in a while, the roof began to leak and the thatch
had to be replaced, but the beams and planks stayed
as strong and beautiful as they were when Bert
first brought them home.

The years went by in their hundreds.

Once, a family raised thirteen children there.
At night they climbed the oaken stairs
and snuggled down to sleep side by side by side,
like a row of peas in a pod.

Through century after century, the oak stayed true.

By and by, a grand new house was built near the cottage.
The furze and heather were cleared away.
A splendid garden was made, with great lawns and curving paths.
Colourful trees and bushes were planted.
Visitors came and peeped in through the cottage windows.

"How quaint!" they said, "Imagine — people actually live here!
Look how wonky the wood is!"

Then there came a time when the grand house lay empty.
An elderly couple lived in the cottage, too frail to tend the gardens.
The forest came creeping back; weedy saplings grew over the lawns.
Brambles and weeds smothered the bushes.
The house and land were divided into lots, to be sold.

"First we'll pull the old cottage down," the owners said,
"nobody will want that. It is finished with."

But on a day of soft mist and rain, when scents from flowers
on the half-smothered trees and plants filled the air,
a young man came walking through the forest. He saw the sad,
neglected cottage and loved it at once.
He bought it, together with the house and the land.

He said, "For hundreds of years the cottage has stood fast against the storms and has sheltered those inside.
It has a story to tell, and the telling is not over.
I will write a new chapter."

He gathered people together and they made a new garden around the old cottage.

Among the ancient trees, they set out winding paths to peaceful, sheltered glades. They planted bright flowers and scented bushes. They made a sparkling water garden, fed from a hidden spring.

They made a place where visitors can find beauty and peace and healing.

They made a place of enchantment.
There are round thatched houses perched
in the trees; shadowy tunnels under bushes,
leading who-knows-where.

Tiny doors have appeared in secret places,
waiting to be found.

They restored the cottage, outside and in,
from the floor to the roof.

They found the oak at its heart.

Now, inside the sheltering walls, young people come to learn,
to work and to grow into the best that they can be.
The cottage rings with their voices and their laughter.

The steadfast oak lives on.

The Furzey Gardens Charitable Trust provides an environment
in which people with learning difficulties can gain real work experience as
part of an educational programme developing independent living skills.

The story of the "Furzey Oak" tells how new life can be found
despite the disasters and difficulties we may face.

We hope that you will enjoy our peaceful paths and glades, finding rest,
refreshment and inspiration in your own way.

For further information see www.furzey-gardens.org
and www.minsteadtrainingproject.org or talk to one of our staff
or students who will be pleased to help you.

Also from the Clucket Press:

Stories by Sandra Horn, illustrated by Karen Popham, set in the Lost Gardens of Heligan in Cornwall.

The Mud Maid is a magical tale of how the Gardens came to be lost and found and restored to life and beauty once again.

Hardcover isbn 13: 978-0-9549256-1-1
Paperback isbn 13: 978-0-9549256-0-4

There's a giant in the woods at the Lost Gardens of Heligan! He found his way there by travelling round the gardens. On his way, he came across all kinds of amazing things, including a pong, a putto, a scarecrow, some stripey buzzers, a hot seat and some spooks! You can see all the places he visited and follow his adventures, until at last you meet him in the spot he likes best of all.

Paperback isbn 13: 978-0-9549256-2-8

and also: a new way to enjoy an old friend!

A cd audiobook of the well-loved story read by the author, complemented by the enchanting songs written by Ruth Kenward for Tattybogle the Musical.

For samples of the music, go to www.starshine.co.uk.

isbn 13: 978-0-9549256-4-2

www.tattybogle.com   **www.mhathaway.co.uk**   **www.karenpopham.co.uk**